Pioneer
Sisters

THE LITTLE HOUSE BOOKS
By Laura Ingalls Wilder
Illustrated by Garth Williams

LITTLE HOUSE IN THE BIG WOODS

LITTLE HOUSE ON THE PRAIRIE

FARMER BOY

ON THE BANKS OF PLUM CREEK

BY THE SHORES OF SILVER LAKE

THE LONG WINTER

LITTLE TOWN ON THE PRAIRIE

THESE HAPPY GOLDEN YEARS

THE FIRST FOUR YEARS

Pioneer Sisters

LAURA INGALLS WILDER

illustrated by
RENÉE GRAEF

HarperCollins*Publishers*

Adaptation by Melissa Peterson.

HarperCollins®, 🏠®, and Little House® are
trademarks of HarperCollins Publishers Inc.

Pioneer Sisters
Text adapted from *Little House on the Prairie* copyright 1935,
copyright renewed 1963, Roger Lea MacBride; *Little House in the Big Woods*
copyright 1932, copyright renewed 1959, Roger Lea MacBride;
The Long Winter copyright 1940, copyright renewed 1968, Roger Lea MacBride.
Illustrations copyright © 1997 by Renée Graef

Library of Congress Cataloging-in-Publication Data
Wilder, Laura Ingalls, 1867–1957.
   Pioneer sisters / Laura Ingalls Wilder ; illustrated by Renée Graef.
      p.   cm. — (A Little house chapter book)
   Summary: Laura Ingalls and her sisters share many adventures while
growing up on the American frontier.
   ISBN 0-06-027132-9 (lib. bdg.) — ISBN 0-06- 442046-9 (pbk.)
   1. Wilder, Laura Ingalls, 1867–1957—Juvenile fiction.   [1. Wilder, Laura
Ingalls, 1867–1957—Fiction.   2. Frontier and pioneer life—Fiction.
3. Sisters—Fiction.   4. Family life—Fiction.]   I. Graef, Renée, ill.   II. Title.
III. Series.
PZ7.W6461Pi   1997   96-11927
[Fic]—dc20   CIP
                                                                          AC

Typography by Alicia Mikles
1   2   3   4   5   6   7   8   9   10
❖
First Edition

Contents

1. In the Big Woods   1

2. A Trip to Town   8

3. Golden Curls, Brown Curls   20

4. On the Prairie   26

5. Fire!   35

6. Plum Creek   41

7. The Straw Stack   51

8. Christmas Surprises   62

CHAPTER 1

In the Big Woods

Laura had two sisters. Mary was the oldest, and Carrie was the youngest. Laura was right in the middle. They all lived with their Pa and Ma in the Big Woods of Wisconsin, in a little gray house made of logs.

All around the house, as far as Laura and Mary could see, were the trees of the Big Woods. There were no other houses, and no other children for them to play with. They played with each other and their good old bulldog, Jack.

The house was small but comfortable. Upstairs there was a big attic. Downstairs was a little bedroom and a big room to live in. There was an iron stove in the big room, and a table and chairs.

In the bedroom was a big bed for Ma and Pa. Mary and Laura slept in a little trundle bed, which was very low to the ground. Every morning Mary and Laura made their bed. Then Ma pushed it out of sight beneath her big bed.

After Mary and Laura made their bed, they wiped the breakfast dishes. Then they helped Ma with the chores. Each day had its own chore. Ma would say:

"Wash on Monday,
Iron on Tuesday,
Mend on Wednesday,
Churn on Thursday,
Clean on Friday,
Bake on Saturday,
Rest on Sunday."

 2

Laura liked the churning day best. Churning meant making butter out of cream. Ma poured cream into a tall pot called a churn. She put a long pole into a hole in the churn lid. The pole was called a dash.

Ma moved the dash up and down, up and down, through the hole. Sometimes she rested, and Mary got to churn for a while. Laura would have liked to help, but the dash was too heavy for her. It took a long, long time for the lump of butter to form in the cream.

After the work was done, Laura and Mary could play. Laura liked noisy games like running and shouting and climbing trees. But Mary liked quiet games like playing house. She was very neat and prim. Laura thought it was more fun to be wild. It was hard to say

3

what Carrie would be like, because she was just a baby.

Mary had a doll named Nettie, a real rag doll, because she was the oldest. Sometimes Mary let Laura hold Nettie, but only when Laura's doll wasn't looking.

Laura's doll was named Susan. She was really just a corncob wrapped in a handkerchief. But she was a good doll anyway. It wasn't her fault she was a corncob.

In the wintertime, when the Big Woods were filled with snow, Mary and Laura stayed inside to play with their dolls. They climbed up to the attic where all kinds of good food was stored. There were huge round pumpkins to use as chairs and tables. Bright red peppers and white onions dangled overhead. There were hams and squashes and good-smelling herbs. Everything was snug and cosy.

 4

In spring, Mary and Laura had playhouses under the two big oak trees in front of the house. Mary had her own tree, and her playhouse was beneath it. Laura's playhouse was under Laura's tree. Each playhouse had a carpet of soft grass. Green leaves made the roofs, and through them Laura and Mary could see bits of sky.

Laura's playhouse had a swing. Pa had hung a slab of bark to a low branch of Laura's tree. That made it Laura's swing, but she had to let Mary swing in it whenever she wanted to.

Mary had a cracked saucer to play with. Laura had a beautiful cup with only one big piece broken out of it. They made little cups and saucers for their dolls out of bits of leaf. Every day the dolls got fresh leaf hats. And Pa made two wooden men to live in the playhouses with the dolls.

Sometimes when Pa came home early he would have time to play with Laura and Mary before supper. One game they loved was called mad dog. Pa would run his fingers through his thick, brown hair, making it stand on end. Then he dropped on all fours and growled. He chased Laura and Mary all around the room.

They were quick at dodging and running away. But once Pa caught them against the wood-box, behind the iron stove. They couldn't get past him. Pa growled a terrible growl. His hair was wild and his eyes were fierce. He was just like a real mad dog.

Mary was so scared she couldn't move. Laura screamed. With a wild leap she scrambled over the wood-box, dragging her big sister with her.

And suddenly there was no mad dog at

all. Just Pa, standing there with his blue eyes shining.

"Well," he said to Laura. "You're only a little half-pint of cider half drunk up, but by Jinks! you're as strong as a little French horse!"

"You shouldn't frighten the children so," Ma said. "Look how big their eyes are."

Pa laughed. He took down his fiddle and began to play and sing. Laura and Mary forgot all about the mad dog. Laura clapped her hands in time as Pa sang out,

"And I'll sing Yankee Doodle-de-do,
And I'll sing Yankee Doodle,
And I'll sing Yankee Doodle-de-do,
And I'll sing Yankee Doodle!"

Mary smiled, Laura clapped, and Baby Carrie cooed in Ma's lap. Nights like that were the best times of all.

CHAPTER 2

A Trip to Town

In the spring, when the crops were in, Pa said it was time for a trip to town. This year, he said, Mary and Laura were old enough to go.

They were very excited. They had never been to town before. Laura had stared at the wagon track that twisted through the woods, wondering what was at the end of it. Now she would find out.

Pa said they would go in a few days. Mary and Laura could hardly wait. They tried to play going to town, but they couldn't do it very well. They weren't sure what a town was like. They knew there was a store in town—but they had never seen one.

Their dolls wanted to go to town too. But Laura and Mary told them, "No, dear, you can't go this year. Perhaps next year, if you are good."

Finally one night Pa said, "We'll go to town tomorrow."

Ma heated water for Laura and Mary's bath, even though it was the middle of the week. Usually bathtime came just once a week, on Saturday night. But a trip to town was a very special occasion.

After they were clean and scrubbed, Ma put up their hair in rag curls. She combed their hair into long wisps and wound each wisp on a bit of rag. When all their hair was wound up, they had knobby little bumps all over their heads. When they went to bed, the little bumps poked into their pillows.

Mary and Laura were so excited that they didn't go to sleep right away. But finally it was morning. They gulped down their breakfast.

Ma took the rags off their hair. She combed so fast that the snarls hurt dreadfully. But it was worth it. Where each rag had been was a long, round curl. Mary had beautiful golden curls, and Laura's ringlets were brown. Baby Carrie didn't have rag curls, because she didn't have much hair yet.

For such an important day they put on their best dresses. Mary's was a china-blue calico. Laura's calico was a lovely dark red. Mary buttoned Laura up the back, and then Ma buttoned Mary.

Pa wore his good shirt. And Ma was

beautiful in her dark brown dress with the little purple flowers all over it.

At last it was time to leave for town. Mary and Laura put on their sunbonnets. Ma put on her hat just as Pa drove the wagon up to the gate.

Ma took Baby Carrie in her arms and sat next to Pa on the wagon seat. Mary and Laura sat behind them on a board nailed across the wagon box. They were happy as they drove through the springtime woods. Carrie laughed and bounced. Pa whistled his happy whistle. The sun was bright and warm on the road.

It was seven miles to town. They drove through the leafy woods filled with sweet, cool smells. Laura and Mary saw rabbits flashing past. They spotted some deer peeking out from between the trees.

Then Laura began to see glimpses of

blue water as blue as the sky through the trees. All at once the road came out of the woods. Ahead was a big lake. It was called Lake Pepin, and the town was built on its shore.

"There you are, Laura and Mary!" Pa said. "There's the town of Pepin."

Laura stood up on the board. Pa held

her safe by the arm so she could see the town. There were so many houses she could hardly breathe. She had never seen anything like it.

Right on the edge of the lake, there was one great big building. Pa told them that was the store. It was not made of logs. It was made of wide, gray boards, running up and down.

Behind it was a clearing where all the trees had been cut down. Standing among the tree stumps were more houses than Laura and Mary could count. In all these houses, people were living. Smoke rose up from their chimneys.

Laura stared. She saw girls and boys playing in the sunshine. She saw someone's laundry spread out to dry on the bushes near a house. She looked and looked, and could not say a word.

13

They left the wagon on the shore of the lake. Pa tied the horses to the wagon box. He took Laura and Mary by the hand. Ma came beside them carrying Baby Carrie. They all walked to the store.

This was where Pa traded his furs. The storekeeper came out from behind the counter and greeted Pa and Ma. Then Laura and Mary had to mind their manners.

"How do you do?" Mary said. But Laura couldn't say anything.

The storekeeper said to Pa and Ma, "That's a pretty little girl you've got there."

He was talking about Mary. He admired her golden curls. He didn't say a word about Laura or her curls, which were the color of plain old dirt.

The store was filled with things to look at! Kegs of nails, sacks of salt, bags of sugar. Big wooden pails full of candy. Boots and knives and tools.

All along one wall were shelves of fabric for making clothes. There were all colors of calico—pinks and blues and reds and browns and purples. Enough for dozens of dresses!

Laura could have looked for weeks. There were so many things to see. She had not known there were so many things in the whole world.

Pa and Ma did their trading. They got tea, and sugar, and cloth for shirts and aprons, and lots of other things. And when the trading was done, the storekeeper gave Mary and Laura each a piece of candy. They were astonished.

They stood staring at their candies. Then Mary remembered her manners.

"Thank you," she said.

Everyone looked at Laura. They were waiting for her to speak, but she could not make a sound. Ma had to ask her, "What do you say, Laura?"

Laura gulped.

"Thank you," she squeaked.

They left the store. Mary and Laura looked at their wonderful candies. They were flat and thin, shaped like hearts. Each candy was white with red letters printed on it. Ma read the words out loud.

Mary's said:

>*Roses are red,*
>*Violets are blue,*
>*Sugar is sweet,*
>*And so are you.*

Laura's said only:

>*Sweets to the sweet.*

 16

Pa led the way back to the wagon. It was time to eat. Ma had brought a picnic dinner. They had bread and butter and cheese, hard-boiled eggs and cookies. They sat on the warm sand watching the waves of Lake Pepin curl and slide at their feet.

After dinner Pa went back to the store. Carrie fell asleep in Ma's arms. Laura and Mary ran along the lake shore, picking up pebbles. There were no pebbles like these back in the Big Woods. They had been rolled back and forth by the waves until they were polished smooth.

When she found a pretty one, Laura put it in her pocket. Each pebble was prettier than the last. Soon she had filled her pocket full.

Pa called out. It was time to go home. Laura ran back to the wagon, her pebbles bouncing in her pocket. Pa picked her up

17

and tossed her into the wagon and then a dreadful thing happened.

The heavy pebbles tore her pocket right out of her dress.

The pebbles clattered all over the wagon box. Laura began to cry. She had torn her best dress.

But Ma said it could be easily fixed. She could sew the pocket back on, good as new.

"Pick up the pretty pebbles, Laura," Ma said. "And next time, don't be so greedy."

Laura gathered up the stones. Pa teased her about taking more than she could carry away.

Nothing like that ever happened to Mary. Mary always kept her dress clean and neat. Mary always minded her manners. Mary had lovely golden curls,

 18

and her candy heart had a poem on it.

Mary looked very good and sweet, sitting on the board next to Laura. Laura didn't think it was fair.

But still, it had been a wonderful day. Laura thought about the wide blue lake, and the town, and the store full of so many good things. She held her pebbles carefully in her lap as the wagon jolted homeward through the Big Woods.

CHAPTER 3

Golden Curls, Brown Curls

One morning Laura was so excited she could hardly stand still while Ma combed her hair. Aunt Lotty was coming!

Mary was already dressed and waiting. Her golden curls shone against her china-blue dress.

Laura liked her own red dress. But her hair was another story. No one noticed plain brown hair. People only made a fuss over Mary's blond curls.

Ma pulled Laura's hair dreadfully as

she combed it into ringlets. Finally she said, "There! Your hair is curled beautifully." She put down the comb. "And Lotty is coming. Run meet her, both of you, and ask her which she likes best, brown curls or golden curls."

Laura and Mary ran out the door and down the path. Aunt Lotty was already at the gate. She wore a beautiful pink dress, and she was swinging a pink sunbonnet by one string.

"Which do you like best, Aunt Lotty," Mary asked, "brown curls, or golden?"

Laura waited to hear what Aunt Lotty would say. She felt miserable.

Aunt Lotty smiled. "I like both kinds best!"

She gave a hand to Laura and a hand to Mary. Together they skipped along to the house, where Ma was waiting.

21

Sunshine streamed through the windows into the house. Everything was neat and pretty. The table was covered with a bright red cloth. Ma had polished the black cookstove till it shone. The pantry door stood wide open, and Laura could smell all the goodies on its shelves.

It was all so nice. Laura felt so happy and good.

After Aunt Lotty went home, Mary and Laura were tired and cross. They went out to the woodpile to gather chips. They hated to pick up chips, but they had to do it every night. Ma needed them to start the fire in the morning. Tonight they hated it more than ever.

Laura snatched up the biggest chip.

"I don't care!" Mary said. "Aunt Lotty likes my hair best, anyway. Golden hair is lots prettier than brown."

Laura's throat swelled tight. She could not speak. Before she knew what she was doing, she reached out and slapped Mary in the face.

"Laura, come here," said a stern voice. It was Pa. He was sitting just inside the door and had seen everything.

Laura went slowly, dragging her feet.

"I told you girls you must never strike each other," Pa said.

"But Mary said—" Laura began.

"That makes no difference. It is what I say that you must mind."

Laura had to be punished. She sat on a chair in the corner and sobbed. When she stopped sobbing, she sulked.

There was only one thing in the whole world to be glad about. Mary had to fill the chip pan all by herself.

At last, when it was getting dark, Pa

said, "Come here, Laura."

His voice was kind. He took Laura on his knee and hugged her close. She snuggled into the crook of his arm and rested her head on his shoulder. Suddenly she felt much better.

She told Pa what Mary had said about her hair. "You don't like golden hair better than brown, do you?" she asked.

Pa's blue eyes shone down at her.

"Well, Laura," he said, smiling, "my hair is brown."

Laura hadn't thought of that. Pa's hair was brown, and his whiskers were brown. She thought brown was a lovely color.

Laura was sorry she hit Mary, but she was still glad that Mary had to gather the chips by herself.

CHAPTER 4

On the Prairie

The Big Woods were filling up with people. New families moved in, cutting down the trees to build houses. There was less room now for the animals that lived in the woods. The deer and the bears and the rabbits were leaving.

Pa decided it was time for the Ingalls family to leave, too. He liked to be in a place where the wild animals could live without being afraid. It was time to move out West.

So the Ingallses packed up all their belongings and rode in a covered wagon all the way to Kansas. Pa built a new log house on the High Prairie. He built a stable for Pet and Patty, their little black horses. Before long Kansas began to feel like home.

The high prairie was as different from the Big Woods as you could get. Back in the woods, there had been nothing but trees as far as the eye could see. Out here on the prairie, there were no trees at all, except for a few down by the river.

Tall yellow grass waved in the wind. Gray-green buffalo grass hugged the ground. Birds flew up out of the grass to soar in the wide blue sky. It was a beautiful place.

Laura and Mary found lots to do on the prairie. Every day, after the beds were made and the dishes washed, they went out to play. They hunted for birds' nests in the tall grass. Whenever they found one, the mother birds squawked and scolded.

Sometimes they lay still as mice to watch prairie chickens play. The little baby chicks ran pecking around their nervous mothers, *cheep cheep cheep*. The smooth brown mothers clucked in warning.

Laura and Mary watched striped snakes rippling through the grass. They had flickering tongues and glittering eyes. They were garter snakes. They wouldn't hurt anybody, but Mary and Laura didn't touch them anyway. Some snakes would bite, and it was better to be safe than sorry.

Sometimes they spotted a big gray rabbit in a clump of grass. The rabbits sat so still in the shadows that Mary and Laura never saw one until they were close enough to touch. But the second they

 28

reached out a hand, the rabbit would bound away in a flash.

The best fun of all was chasing gophers. The little brown striped animals lived in holes all over the prairie. They would pop up out of a hole and stand on their hind legs to look at Laura and Mary. They had bright round eyes and

crinkling noses. Their fur looked soft as velvet.

Mary and Laura wanted to catch one and give him to Ma. But they could never get close enough. A gopher would stand perfectly still until they were sure they had him. Then, just as Mary or Laura touched him—pop!—he wasn't there. There was just his round hole in the ground.

One afternoon Pa took Mary and Laura to see an Indian camp. The Indians had moved on, but there was lots to see in the place they had lived. There were ashes where campfires had been. There were holes in the ground where tent-poles had been driven. Bones were scattered where Indian dogs had gnawed them.

All around the camp, the grasses were bitten short. The Indian ponies had grazed

 30

there. Tracks were everywhere—tracks of big moccasins, little moccasins, even tracks of little bare toes.

Suddenly Laura shouted, "Look! Look!"

Something bright glittered in the dust. It was a beautiful blue bead. Laura picked it up, shouting with joy.

Then Mary saw a red bead. Laura spotted a green one. They forgot everything but beads. Pa helped them look.

They found white beads and brown beads. They found more and more red and blue beads. All that afternoon they hunted for beads in the dust of the Indian camp.

At last they couldn't find any more. Laura had a handful of beads. So did Mary. Pa tied the beads into his handkerchief. Laura's beads were in one corner, Mary's in the other.

When they got home, Pa tossed the handkerchief to Ma.

"Look what the girls found," he said.

Ma untied the handkerchief. She gasped when she saw the beads. They were even prettier than they'd been in the camp.

Laura stirred her beads with a finger. She watched them sparkle and shine.

"These are mine," she said.

Then Mary said, "Carrie can have mine."

Ma looked at Laura. Laura didn't say anything. She wanted to keep those pretty beads. She wished with all her might that Mary wouldn't always be such a good girl.

But she couldn't let Mary be better than she was. She said slowly, "Carrie can have mine, too."

"That's my unselfish, good little girls," Ma said.

She poured Mary's beads into Mary's hands. She poured Laura's into Laura's hands. She said she'd give them a thread to string them on. The beads would make a pretty necklace for Carrie to wear.

Mary and Laura sat side by side on their bed. They strung the bright beads onto the thread, one by one. They didn't talk.

Maybe Mary felt sweet and good inside, but Laura didn't. When she looked at Mary, she wanted to slap her. So she didn't dare look at Mary again.

The beads made a beautiful necklace. Carrie clapped her hands and laughed when she saw it. Ma tied the necklace around Carrie's little neck. It glittered there, and Laura felt a tiny bit better. After all, her beads were not enough beads to make a whole necklace, and neither were Mary's. But together they made a whole string for Carrie.

Laura often thought about the walk across the prairie and about all they had seen at the Indian camp. The prairie held so many surprises.

CHAPTER 5

Fire!

The prairie began to change. The green grass turned yellow and the yellow grass turned brown. The wind wailed like someone crying. Fall had come.

The weather was cooler now. Pa cut firewood down at the creek. He stacked it against the house. There was enough wood to last all winter. Down by the creek the trees were changing colors. The leaves turned red and yellow and brown.

One afternoon a fierce wind blew in. It was too cold to play outside anymore. Ma called Mary and Laura into the house. She built up the fire and pulled the rocking chair close to it.

Ma took Baby Carrie into her lap. She sat rocking, singing softly to the baby,

"By lo, baby bunting.

Papa's gone a-hunting,

To get a rabbit skin

To wrap the baby bunting in."

Suddenly Laura heard a crackling noise. It was coming from the chimney.

Ma stopped singing. She looked up inside the chimney. Then she got up quietly and handed the baby to Mary. She pushed Mary down into the rocking chair and hurried out of the house.

Laura ran after her. They stared up at the chimney. It was on fire! The sticks that made it were burning up. The fire roared in the wind. It was about to

 36

spread to the roof.

Ma grabbed a long pole. She struck and struck at the roaring fire. Burning sticks fell all around her.

Laura didn't know what to do. She grabbed a pole too. But Ma told her to stay away.

The roaring fire was terrible. It could burn the whole house down, and there was nothing Laura could do.

She ran into the house. Burning sticks and coals were falling down the chimney. The house was full of smoke.

A big, blazing stick rolled onto the floor—right underneath Mary's skirt. Mary was so scared she couldn't move.

Laura grabbed the back of the heavy rocking-chair. She pulled with all her might. The chair, with Mary and Carrie in it, slid backward across the floor.

In a flash, Laura grabbed up the
burning stick. She threw it into the fireplace just as Ma came in.

"Good girl, Laura," Ma said. She took
the water-pail and poured water on the
fireplace. Clouds of steam rose up. The
fire was out.

Ma turned to Laura.

"Did you burn your hands?" she asked.

She looked at Laura's palms. They weren't burned. Laura had been too fast for that.

Laura was too big to cry. Only one tear ran out of each eye and her throat choked up, but that wasn't crying. She hid her face against Ma and hung on tight.

Ma stroked Laura's hair.

"Were you afraid?" she asked.

"Yes," Laura said. "I was afraid Mary and Carrie would burn up. I was afraid the house would burn up and we wouldn't have any house!"

Mary told Ma how Laura had pulled the chair away from the fire. Ma was surprised. Laura was so little, and the chair was so big and heavy. With Mary and Carrie in it, it was even heavier. Ma said she didn't know how Laura had done it.

"You were a brave girl, Laura," she said. But Laura had really been terribly scared.

39

"And no harm's done," Ma said. "The house didn't burn up, and Mary's skirts didn't catch fire and burn her and Carrie. So everything is all right."

When Pa came home from hunting, the house was cold. The wind was roaring over the stone part of the chimney. The tall stick part had all burned away. But Pa said he would build up the chimney with green sticks that wouldn't burn. He'd plaster it well so it would never catch fire again.

He gave Ma the four fat ducks he had shot. Then he went whistling outside to cut green sticks for the new chimney. Soon a new fire crackled merrily and the warm smell of cornbread filled the house. Ma cleaned the ducks and put one to roast on the hearth.

Everything was snug and cozy again.

 40

Plum Creek

Spring came. It was time to move again. The government had decided that Pa's land belonged to the Indians. Once more Pa and Ma loaded up the covered wagon with all their belongings and the Ingallses set off to find a new place to settle.

Laura was excited. You never knew what would happen next, or where you'd be tomorrow, when you traveled in a covered wagon.

Pet and Patty pulled the wagon all the way across Kansas. They pulled it across Missouri and across Iowa. They pulled it a long way into Minnesota, and there they stopped.

Pa bought a house and some land. It was the funniest house Laura and Mary had ever seen. It was called a dugout.

A big hole had been dug into the side of a creek bank. It had a regular wooden door, but the walls were dirt. The ceiling was made of hay.

There was a little path leading from the house up to the prairie. Laura and Mary could walk up the path and stand right on the roof of their house. It didn't look like a roof at all. It was just a piece of ground with grass growing on it.

Inside, the house was clean and neat. The walls were whitewashed. The dirt floor was smooth and hard. This was Laura and Mary's new home.

The little path that led up to the

prairie also went down to the creek. Plum Creek was a wonderful place for Mary and Laura to play. Every morning they did the dishes, made their bed, and swept the floor. Then they ran outside to the creek.

Sometimes they waded in the shallow water. The mud of the creek bottom was cool on their feet. Silvery fish nibbled and tickled around their toes.

On top of the water, water-bugs skated. They had long legs. Their feet made tiny dents in the water. Water-bugs skated so fast that almost before Mary and Laura saw one it was somewhere else.

All along the creek bank grew tall, round rushes. They were little hollow tubes that fitted together at joints. When Laura and Mary pulled on them, the rushes squeaked. The tubes squeaked when you pulled them apart. They squeaked when you pushed them together again.

Laura and Mary made necklaces out of the little tubes. They blew through big tubes and made the water bubble. They scared the little fishes by blowing at them. When Laura and Mary were thirsty, they used the tubes like straws to drink the cool water of the creek.

Ma laughed whenever Mary and Laura came in all splashed and muddy from the creek. They wore green necklaces and carried long green wands made of rushes.

"I declare," Ma said, "you two play in the creek so much, you'll be turning into water-bugs!"

One day Laura and Mary were standing in the creek, letting the minnows nibble at their toes. Suddenly Laura saw a strange creature in the water.

"What's that!" Mary said. She was scared.

The creature was almost as long as Laura's foot. In front he had two long arms that ended in big claws. Along his sides were short legs, and he had a strong, flat tail. His eyes were round and bulging. Bristles stuck out of his nose.

He was a crab. Laura slowly bent down to see him better. Faster than a water-bug, he shot backward and disappeared. A little curl of water came out from under a flat rock where he had gone.

Laura and Mary stared at the rock. In a minute the old crab stuck out a claw and snapped it. Then he peeked out.

Laura waded nearer. The crab flipped backward under the stone. But when Laura splashed water at the stone, he ran out, snapping his claws. Laura screamed.

Mary shrieked. They ran splashing away from the crab's home, laughing and screaming.

They found a big stick and went back to the flat rock. Laura poked the stick at the rock. The crab reached out a claw. *Snap!* He broke the stick right in two.

Laura and Mary found a bigger stick. This time the crab clamped hold of it and did not let go. Laura lifted him out of the water. His eyes glared. *Snap! Snap!* went his other claw. Then he let go and dropped. He flipped under his stone again.

Every time Laura and Mary splashed his stone, the crab came snapping out. He was fighting mad. It was great fun to run screaming away from his clicking claws.

After a while Laura and Mary went wading again. They walked upstream to a place where plum trees grew along the banks. The water near the trees was dark and muddy.

Mary didn't like to wade in mud. She sat on the bank while Laura splashed in the dark water.

The mud squelched between Laura's

47

toes. It came up in clouds till she couldn't see the bottom of the creek. The air smelled old and musty. Laura waded back into the clean water and the sunshine.

She saw some dark blobs on her legs and feet. They looked like mud. She splashed clear water over them, but they did not wash away.

She tried to scrape them off with her hand. They wouldn't come off.

The blobs were the color of mud. They were soft like mud. But they stuck as tight as Laura's skin.

Laura screamed. "Oh, Mary, Mary! Come quick!"

Mary came, but she wouldn't touch the horrible blobs. She said they were worms. Worms made her sick.

Worms! Laura felt sick too. She felt sicker than Mary. But it was more awful to have those things on her than it was to touch them. She dug into one with her fingernails and pulled.

The thing stretched out long— longer—longer still. But it kept holding on.

"Oh, don't!" Mary cried. "You'll pull it in two!"

But Laura kept pulling. She pulled it longer and longer, till finally it snapped off.

Blood trickled down her leg from where the thing had been.

Laura looked at the other blobs. One by one, she pulled them off. A little trickle of blood ran down where each one let go.

Laura didn't feel like playing anymore. She washed the blood off her legs. She rinsed her hands in the clean water. Then she walked back home with Mary.

Laura told Pa and Ma about the blobs.

Ma said they were leeches. Doctors put them on sick people.

Pa called them bloodsuckers. He said they lived in the mud, in dark, still places in the water.

"I don't like them," Laura said. Mary agreed.

Pa laughed. "Then stay out of the mud, flutterbudget!" he said. "If you don't want trouble, don't go looking for it."

CHAPTER 7

The Straw Stack

One late summer morning Mary and Laura went up on the prairie to play. The first thing they saw was a tall golden straw-stack.

Pa had made it. He had piled straw up into a huge shining heap. The cattle would be able to eat the straw all winter long.

Mary and Laura stared at the straw-stack. It was beautiful. The sun shone brightly on the yellow straw. It smelled sweeter than hay.

Laura ran straight to the stack and

began to climb. Her feet slid in the slippery straw. But she could climb faster than straw slid, and in a minute she was high on top of the stack.

She looked around at the great, round, wide prairie. She was high up in the sky, almost as high as birds. Her feet bounced on the springy straw.

She waved her arms in the air. She was almost flying, way up high in the windy air.

"I'm flying! I'm flying!" she called down to Mary. Mary climbed up to her.

"Jump!" Laura said. They held hands and jumped, round and round. Higher and higher they jumped. The wind blew and their skirts flapped. Their sunbonnets swung on their strings.

"Higher! Higher!" Laura sang. She jumped as high as she could.

Suddenly the straw slid under her. She

slipped over the edge of the stack and slid faster and faster all the way to the bottom.

Bump! She landed at the foot of the stack.

Plump! Mary landed on top of her.

They laughed and laughed. The straw crackled all around them. Then they climb the stack again and slid back down. They had never had so much fun. It was even better than playing in the creek.

They climbed and slid, climbed and slid, over and over. The straw-stack got smaller and smaller. Soon there was hardly any stack left at all—just loose heaps of straw on the ground.

Laura looked at Mary. Mary looked at Laura. Pa had worked hard to make that straw-stack. Now it was not at all as he had left it.

Mary said she was going into the

dugout. Laura went quietly with her. They were very good, helping Ma and playing nicely with Carrie.

And then Pa came in to dinner.

He looked straight at Laura. Laura looked at the floor.

"You girls mustn't slide down the straw-stack any more," Pa said. "I had to pile it all back up again."

"We won't, Pa," Laura promised.

Mary nodded. "No, Pa, we won't."

After dinner Mary washed the dishes and Laura dried them. Then they put on their sunbonnets. They walked along the path to the prairie.

The straw-stack was golden-bright in the sunshine. Laura walked up to it and stood very close.

"Laura!" Mary cried. "What are you doing!"

"I'm not doing anything!" Laura said. "I'm not hardly even touching it!"

"You come right away from there, or I'll tell Ma!" Mary said.

"Pa didn't say I couldn't smell it," Laura argued.

She leaned close to the straw. She sniffed long, deep sniffs. The straw was warm in the sun. It smelled better than wheat kernels taste when you chew them.

Laura buried her face in the warm straw. She sniffed deeper and deeper.

"Mmm!"

Mary came and smelled it too. "Mmm!"

Laura looked up at the golden straw-stack. She had never seen the sky so blue as it was above that gold. She just could not stay on the ground. She had to be high up in that blue sky.

She began to climb.

"Laura!" Mary cried. "Pa said we mustn't!"

"He did not!" Laura said. "He didn't say we mustn't climb up it—he said we mustn't slide down it. I'm only climbing!"

"You come right straight down from there," said Mary.

By now Laura was on top of the stack. She looked down at Mary.

"I am not going to slide down," she said in her best good-girl voice. "Pa said not to."

She was higher than everything. Everything except that blue, blue sky. The wind was blowing. The wide green prairie stretched out beneath her.

Laura spread her arms. She jumped into the air. The springy straw bounded her high.

 56

"I'm flying! I'm flying!" she sang.

That did it. Mary wanted to fly, too. She climbed up to join Laura.

They bounced and bounced. They bounced until they could go no higher. Then they flopped flat on the sweet warm straw.

Bulges of straw rose up on both sides of Laura. She rolled onto a bulge and it sank. But another rose up beside her.

She rolled onto that bulge, and another one. And then she was rolling faster and faster. She couldn't stop.

"Laura!" Mary screamed. "Pa said—"

But Laura was rolling. Over, over, right down the whole straw-stack she rolled. She thumped in straw on the ground.

She jumped up and climbed the stack again.

"Come on, Mary!" she shouted. "Pa didn't say we can't roll!" She began to roll again.

Mary stayed on top of the stack. "I know Pa didn't say we can't roll," she said, "but—"

"Well then!" Laura climbed up and rolled down again.

"Come on!" she called up. "It's lots of fun!"

"Well, but I—" said Mary. Then she came rolling down.

It was great fun. It was more fun than sliding. They climbed and rolled, climbed and rolled. More and more straw rolled down with them. They waded in it and climbed and rolled. They rolled until there was hardly anything left to climb.

Then they brushed every bit of straw off their dresses. They picked every bit of

 58

straw out of their hair. They went quietly into the dugout.

That night, when Pa came in from the fields, he said, "Laura, come here."

Slowly Laura went to stand by Mary.

Pa looked at Laura. He said, sternly, "You girls have been sliding down the straw-stack again."

"No, Pa," said Laura.

"Mary!" said Pa. "Did you slide down the straw-stack?"

"N-no, Pa," Mary said.

"Laura!" Pa's voice was terrible. "Tell me again, DID YOU SLIDE DOWN THE STRAW-STACK?"

"No, Pa," Laura answered again. She looked straight into Pa's shocked eyes. She didn't know why he looked like that.

"Laura!" Pa said.

"We didn't slide down it, Pa," Laura

 60

explained. "But we did roll down it."

Pa got up quickly. He went to the door and stood looking out. His back shook. Laura and Mary didn't know what to think.

Pa turned around. His face was stern, but his eyes twinkled.

"All right, Laura," he said. "But now I want you girls to stay away from that straw-stack. Pete and Bright and Spot need every bite of it to eat this winter. You don't want them to be hungry, do you?"

"Oh, no, Pa!" they said.

"Well, if that straw's to be fit to feed them, it MUST—STAY—STACKED. Do you understand?"

"Yes, Pa," said Laura and Mary.

That was the end of their playing on the straw-stack.

CHAPTER 8

Christmas Surprises

Christmas was coming. The sky turned gray, and the wind was cold. Laura and Mary began to wonder about Santa Claus. How could he visit the dugout when there was no chimney for him to climb down?

Mary asked Ma about it. Ma didn't answer. Instead, she asked, "What do you girls want for Christmas?"

Laura looked up from the table, where she was making an apron for her doll. "I want candy," she said.

"So do I," said Mary.

"Tandy?" cried Baby Carrie. She was playing by herself on Ma and Pa's bed.

"And a new winter dress," Mary went on. "And a coat and a hood."

"So do I," said Laura.

Ma took the iron off the stove where it had been heating. She began to iron one of Pa's shirts. "Do you know what Pa wants for Christmas?" she asked.

Mary and Laura did not know.

"Horses," Ma said. "Would you girls like that?"

They didn't answer.

"I only thought," Ma said, "if we all wished for horses, and nothing but horses, then maybe—"

Laura and Mary looked at each other. They knew what Ma wanted them to do.

If they wished for nothing but horses,

that's what Santa would bring. No candy, no dresses, no new winter coats.

They looked at each other again, then quickly looked away. They didn't say anything.

Even Mary, who was always so good, did not say a word.

But that night after supper, Laura went to Pa.

"Pa, I want Santa Claus—to bring—"

"What?" Pa asked.

"Horses," said Laura. "If you will let me ride them sometimes."

"So do I!" Mary chimed in. But Laura had said it first.

Pa was surprised. His eyes shone soft and bright.

"Would you girls really like horses?" he asked.

"Oh yes, Pa!" they answered.

 64

That settled it. They would not have any Christmas, only horses.

Laura tried to feel glad about it. But it would feel strange not to have any presents at all on Christmas morning.

Carrie was too little to understand about the horses. And the next day, when Carrie was asleep, Ma called Mary and Laura to her side. Her face was shining with a secret. There would be one Christmas present, after all. Mary and Laura could make Carrie a button-string!

Laura and Mary would have to make it while Carrie was napping. They climbed onto their bed, keeping their backs to their little sister.

Ma brought them her button-box. She had saved buttons since she was smaller than Laura. The box was almost full. Mary and Laura spread the buttons out on their skirts.

There were blue buttons and red buttons. Silver ones and gold ones. Buttons with castles and bridges and trees on them. Shiny black buttons, striped buttons, painted china buttons.

There were buttons that looked like real blackberries, fat and juicy. And one tiny button made Laura squeal when she saw it. It was in the shape of a little dog's head.

"Sh!" Ma warned. But Carrie didn't wake up.

Some of the buttons were even older than Ma. Ma's mother had saved them when she was a little girl. Ma gave them all those buttons, even the dog's-head one, to make a button-string for Carrie.

After that it was fun to stay in the dugout while the cold wind roared outside. Mary and Laura had a secret.

It was hard to keep Carrie from finding out. When she was awake, Laura and Mary played with her and gave her everything she wanted. They cuddled her and sang to her. Mostly they tried to get her to sleep. Then they worked on the button-string.

Mary had one end of the string. Laura had the other. They picked out the best buttons and strung them on the string.

They held the string out to look at it. Sometimes they took off buttons and put

on others. They wanted to make the most beautiful button-string in the world.

Christmas Eve came. They had to finish the button-string today.

But they couldn't get Carrie to sleep. She ran and shouted. She climbed on benches and jumped off. She skipped and sang. The only thing she didn't do was get tired.

Mary told her to sit still like a little lady. But Carrie wouldn't listen.

Laura let Carrie hold her doll. Carrie bounced the poor doll up and down and threw her against the wall. And still Carrie didn't get sleepy.

Finally Ma took Carrie into her lap. Ma began to sing in a sweet, low voice. Laura and Mary were perfectly still. Ma's voice got lower and lower. Carrie's eyes blinked till they shut. Ma let her song fade away.

Carrie's eyes popped open.

"More! More!" she shouted.

Ma sang and sang. And at last Carrie fell asleep. Then quickly, quickly, Laura and Mary finished the button-string.

Ma tied the ends together for them. It was beautiful.

That evening after supper, when Carrie was sound asleep, Ma hung her little baby stockings from the edge of the table. Laura and Mary, in their nightgowns, slipped the button-string into one stocking.

Then they began to climb in bed. Pa said, "Aren't you girls going to hang your stockings?"

"But," Laura said, "I thought Santa Claus was going to bring us horses."

"Maybe he will," Pa said. "But little girls always hang up their stockings on Christmas Eve, don't they?"

Laura didn't know what to think.

Neither did Mary. They had wished hard for nothing but horses, and horses wouldn't fit in a stocking.

Ma took two clean stockings out of the clothes-box. Pa hung them beside Carrie's. Laura and Mary said their prayers and went to sleep, wondering.

In the morning Laura heard the fire crackling. She opened one eye. In the light of the lamp, she could see a bulge in her Christmas stocking.

She squealed and jumped out of bed. Mary came running, too.

Laura looked in her stocking. Inside was a little paper package. Mary had one just like it.

The packages were filled with candy. Laura had six pieces, and Mary had six. They had never seen such beautiful candy. It was too beautiful to eat.

Some pieces were like ribbons, bent in waves.

Some were short bits of round stick candy. On their flat ends were colored flowers that went all the way through.

Some pieces were perfectly round, with stripes on them.

Carrie had some candy too. In one of her stockings were four of the beautiful pieces.

And in the other stocking was the button-string. When Carrie saw it, her eyes and mouth grew round. She squealed and grabbed the string. The beautiful buttons glittered in the lamplight. The juicy blackberry buttons looked good enough to eat. The tiny dog's head winked and shone.

Carrie squealed again. She wriggled and laughed with joy. Mary and Laura were glad they had worked so hard to make the button-string.

Pa said, "Do you suppose there is anything for us in the stable?"

"Dress as fast as you can, girls," said Ma. "Go to the stable and see what Pa finds."

They put on their stockings and shoes. They wrapped themselves in warm shawls and ran out into the cold.

Pa stood waiting in the stable door. He laughed when he saw Laura and Mary all bundled up.

Standing in the stable were two horses. Their red-brown hair shone like silk. They had black manes and black tails. Their eyes were bright and gentle.

Laura held out a hand. The horses put their velvety noses down and nibbled softly on it. Their breath was warm.

"Well, flutterbudget!" said Pa. "And Mary. How do you girls like your Christmas?"

 72

"Very much, Pa," said Mary.

Laura could only gasp, "Oh, Pa!"

Pa's eyes shone deep. "Who wants to ride the Christmas horses?" he asked.

Laura could hardly wait. Pa lifted Mary up and showed her how to hold on to the mane. Then his strong hands swung Laura onto the other horse's back.

The horse felt warm and strong beneath Laura. She could feel its aliveness carrying her. Pa led the way down to the creek. The horses pricked their velvety ears forward and backward.

Laura looked at her sister. They were so happy they had to laugh. Inside the warm dugout, Carrie had her button-string—the most beautiful button-string in the world. And out here, in the bright morning sun, Laura and Mary were riding the wonderful Christmas horses.